HANDS FOR LANGUAGE

Uma Menon

MAWENZI
HOUSE

We acknowledge the support of the Canada Council for the Arts for our publishing program. We also acknowledge support from the Government of Ontario through the Ontario Arts Council, and the support of the Government of Canada through the Canada Book Fund.

ONTARIO ARTS COUNCIL
CONSEIL DES ARTS DE L'ONTARIO
an Ontario government agency
un organisme du gouvernement de l'Ontario

Canada Council for the Arts Conseil des arts du Canada

Canada

Cover design by Sabrina Pignataro
Cover art: Nadia Grapes / Abstract floral seamless pattern with trendy hand drawn textures. Modern abstract design for paper, cover, fabric, interior decor and other users / Shutterstock

Library and Archives Canada Cataloguing in Publication

Title: Hands for language / Uma Menon.
Names: Menon, Uma, 2003- author.
Description: Poems.

Identifiers: Canadiana (print) 20200261258 | Canadiana (ebook) 20200261304 | ISBN 9781774150085
(softcover) | ISBN 9781774150092 (EPUB) | ISBN 9781774150108 (PDF)
Classification: LCC PS3613.E555 H36 2020 | DDC 811/.6—dc23

Printed and bound in Canada by Coach House Printing

Mawenzi House Publishers Ltd.
39 Woburn Avenue (B)
Toronto, Ontario M5M 1K5
Canada

www.mawenzihouse.com

CONTENTS

part one: birth

prelude

as a portrait of mother on the terrace

up there is   a secret
a memory   a loss
a sin   a clothespin
that   unclips
my mother   loose
in the wind & leaves
her hollowed   a tree
some wood   some
cotton   a hole
in   the thread of her
wind-birthed   skirt
is a   child's hand
& a prayer of   a kiss
a maiden   a soldier
a damsel   in
stress   she tells all
the world   her
beloved   is here

citizenship

my first country smelled like jasmine flowers
        grown from the earth   her roots
were the first things i held with my small fists
& her breath   was the first prayer i repeated
my mother tells me that i cried   when i left
my first country: maybe it was just
the jasmine or maybe it was the fear
of naturalization   to another country or
        another identity   or maybe
because my mother   would never be
my country   again

aubade

it is still dawn when i rise   to the voice   of an untranslatable
prayer   & worship the rain that strokes the roof
in the dark   my mother tells me of a peacock singing in the rain
i cannot hear it but i wonder   if i may speak to it
my wet hair is wrapped in a towel & i imagine the rain washing
away my body   my fear   & leaving atop a feather
i follow blue with my nose & feel beads dance   through my
fingers in quiet so my grandmother may sleep   like her prayers

here i learn to make food with only   my hands   not because
i am a woman   but despite   being a woman
here i find two women & one girl rising before dawn in their own
home not because they are homesick   but because they will be
here is the place where they were born one morning   like this
where they said their first prayer   & made their first morning
here is the place where i never lived but called home   because
my mother did   & my grandmother did   in their prayers

birthdays

my fifth birthday was the first one i learned to remember
the dress i wore   the meal i ate   the people who
carried me in their arms like an angel
        the way the wind swept me up   like its child
when i opened the terrace   & how i cupped my ear
when the rain promised to tell me why it wept   each day

my fifteenth birthday was the first time   that i wondered
why we celebrate the day we leave   our mothers' bodies
& mourn the day when   we leave our own

origin story

in which parasurama throws an axe to uncover a land
& i become landless

here   he stands   here   falls his axe
                & here:
                  i call home

here
the blood of kshatriyas dissolves
into salt & covers a land
blood runs through this land   or
salt gnaws through this land

this land is his own &
this land is my mother's gift

my fingers   too   wield an axe
with teeth at the end squared away
growling in defense of my land &
in fear of myself

ode to a previous life

this is the way that
sunshine wilts:
it gives way to the flowers
who breathe no longer

i was once the daughter of an ocean
too afraid   to be swallowed
            by my own blood
that instead   i became a fish
in the next life
the men i fear appear in my dreams
            to take me back
to the darkest lair   where my nose
was pierced   by a hunter's spear

it is my fear of drowning   that has
brought me here   to watch my fears
dissolve &
renew—
to become a trident &
to become a fish in this one body
in this one life
as i fall   from the ocean's depths
to this corner of the earth
i hear her say that the mountains
                                        are my sisters
it is with pain   that i become
my own ancestor &
shed the skin   that was once mine

at the intersection of the land & the sea

the story goes that my mother's land
was born from the fall of an axe &
my mother was born from the rise
of a sailing ship

her feet are planted where the land
meets the ocean
in circles

each sunset, her eyes meet the sun &
one day before i was born—
like this—
she told me that we
are just tumbleweed
so i fall into the ocean & grow no feet
to drown with

my mother draws numbers all day &
sometimes she cannot tell—only count
count again
& again
recount
what she left behind
my mother cannot swim:

her feet are too stiff
to draw circles in the ocean
but her body has hollowed
enough to fly across the sea
a thousand times through
the sun
she says we

are an empty people—
                    our bodies filled
with the weight of incense &
this is why we sink
            not float

my mother thought this country
was a language
so she made a voice out of its teeth &
filled her ears with the driest of soil

she fears that one day
my tongue will become
a barren land—
            arid & incapable

what she didn't understand
was that it was the ocean
            not the land
who mothered a language

my biggest fear isn't
knowing where i am from
            instead
it is knowing
where i am not
from

the creation of a language

a language spreads itself thin
across the oceans &
i become its water

my first language was born in a land
cut from the plentiful sea &
mid-sentence an axe falls

my tongue becomes its own language
with teeth to cut grammar &
lips to spell in silence

my first language became a mother
before i was born &
i became a tongue

leaving milwaukee

field full of wishes
& a breath
too weak to keep

the sun has strewn
its clothes
across the midday sky

my hair—
dandelions,
sewn in place,

my lips
of lilacs plucked
as décor

we are falling
with hands
gripping our mouths

lilacs &
dandelions
on concrete slabs

the empty streets
won't take me
home,

but a cloudy hourglass
might keep me
silent

coming home

outside the gates,
a cow empties herself

to feed her child &
tonight we are churning
butter with our hands.

salt always nips
at my tongue
so that wherever i am,
it must not be home.

the wind, loudest
at dawn, races past me

to rectify its own &
whips up butter before
it reaches my throat.
today, i am building

a house: with its four walls
made of hands & its roof
of salted butter.

when the roof melts
on my tongue, the hands
tighten their grip
till i find

that my own house
has strangled me whole.

out

it is night now & the lights are nothing but songs
in the wind: there   but not here

so we say our prayers to a room we believe   but
do not see   in this outage

i trace the handle of an oil lamp with my finger
& pinch the grease along my thumb   imagining

a genie   emerging from the mouth of the tired lamp
spitting another body   & swallowing me instead

i rub my hair between my fingers to implant this oil
& turn away   this kindling

i rub a genie between my teeth as a wish & i wave a finger
through this air   as a goodbye   to the lightless

part two: discovery

spoken language

my uncle tells me that he can speak   with his hands
& asks me   to translate his words into malayalam
i listen carefully: the rain weeps outside & the terrace
lies open   unafraid both   of men who speak
with their mouths   & men who speak with
their roughened hands   in the shadows
a billowed body dances with his hands   against
the wall where fingers trace wind   & currents deflect
air   *here is a secret* he says with his blundering
mouth & rolls his fist across the table   my eyes
flicker like lights before i see   what he has shown me

i forget

the first time i forget how to say *shoulder* in malayalam
my mother's face caves in fear & her honey forehead
streaks in confusion *this is not how she taught me*
to forget this is not how she taught me to bend my
words bend the muscles of my mouth bend in two to
carry malayalam & english in my two palms *& now*
i have forgotten where my arms bend to form wilting stems
& now that i have unshouldered malayalam i must
carry this lump at the base of my throat

the universe, a woman

(i) prologue

they say the universe formed with one big bang but
we all know it must have a mother.
listen to the theory of maternal relativity,
find power to expand. the blood
of the universe has turned cold in search
of its mother.

(ii) galaxies

there was a time when my path was enshrined,
when you worshipped my footsteps, gravitating
towards each of my movements. call it a galaxy.
there was a time when you savored the milk i spilled
and bottled it up like a genie for posterity to stare
and wonder at.
there was a time when you looked up at the sky
& saw only my light. you prayed to me
& divinity.

(iii) nebula

they say that when woman is angry
she devours the whole world.
they are wrong, of course—
she devours the entire universe.
all that is left is dust,
dust in more colors than emotions felt

when i swallow you whole.
my fingers are the pillars of creation
that give you this life. i birth the stars you sing of.
orbit me. feel ego dissipate into dust,
dust.

akbar & birbal count crows

he says he knew it all along   the same way
he knew the number of crows in the kingdom
before counting them   a census
reports   that girls are now becoming crows
their hands parched by plastic dolls   are now
becoming soot wings that men   won't
approve of   akbar might not anyways
imagining his firstborn daughter   ballooning
through the sky to touch a crow   maybe
she was one of the 95,463 that birbal reported
        maybe   birbal knew that   too

my grandmother's jewelry

she lays a platter of chains in front of me
the kind that detach that connect that
won't break when my hands become
razor-speech
they just lie there as pointed words do
when it is too cold to multiply
my grandmother's eyes lie upon me
fixed to the gold asking me to pick
a color pick a shape pick a luster to bury
my ash body
this is what my skin would look like
if it shone
but my eyes disarm stop to pass through
the plastic crystals
how is it that india is home to so many
snow-diamonds
& i am still the color
of shineless gold

(mother earth) giving birth to trees

at the floor of her stomach lies
a limb reaching upward

trying to console the withering
body that gave it this life

when child dies in heat
mother searches for a light

to avenge murder by a certain
breed of two-legged creatures

roots born to always hold on
to a mother's gentle grasp

blessed without feet to pick up
& disown the touch of earth

when her flesh is peeled away
& wrinkles sold limited-edition

tears fall from a child's face
as rage-dusted leaves in an autumn

of celebration
& warmth

the world lies between her two eyes

in my dreams   a woman appears to tell me
what will happen next summer   she has the same
venus-flytrap-eyes as my mother
ready to swallow lies / even when closed / & tell
truths that taste like lies   *this is it*   she says
when everything looks like the insides   of a venus
flytrap   *here is your body*   *& the world is*
coming closer   my mother's eyes fall together
with my knees   & together we watch   the end
clutched between her fingers

trusting the birds

it is raining outside when amma
runs out of clothespins: the wind,
unforgiving in its embrace, blows
a cave into a wet sari   *better than*
moth holes   i tell myself when
a black kite turns to soot   *& it's*
just a bird   there is a clothespin
at the end of each of its talons but
they latch only on to
                    aren't you afraid

amma tells the story of the dress
that flew away   *with so much air*
in the pockets & i can't help but
think of the birds   carrying away
my shawl   when the trees are
all gone, split into wood to make
clothespins   *the cloth will make*
for good nesting material   it is
still raining here   so amma & i
become clothespins   clutching
afghan blankets between our nails

girl growing up in the south enters the midwest

a tall man lightly chuckles
when i tug the bus cord. he sees
my sunburnt fingers: deep
brown, but inside a tender red.
empathy is fresh, i overhear
at the lunch counter.
i'm pulling the tomatoes out
of my sandwich—cheese,
lettuce, and soupy beans.
in the midwest, vegetarians
are the tomatoes: picked
before ripe & tossed into
sandwiches. once,
in milwaukee, i forgot how
to speak. the restaurant owner tells me
not to worry & instead
hands me a check. i'm learning
to be grateful. the strawberries here
taste better than in florida. fresher,
even.

dictionary: tanpura

noun

1. string instrument that cannot
   play a melody

say a long-necked lute
has been strung out
in the sun
its songs worn & ripped
like clothes
its neck manhandled
its strings plucked away
i am searching for the tool
that turns wood into
instruments

2. instrument that provides
   a harmonic drone

i imagine it
as an unmanned vehicle
over my head / as a man
spitting syllables
i say i know what it's like
to be called names
to be named & renamed
but she doesn't flinch

giving a mongoose a plastic bottle

in my motherland, i see
a mongoose sinking
its warrior teeth into plastic trash.
the sunlight reflects its struggle,
plastic across the oceans, across
rice fields, across a cardboard
building where a forest
once breathed. this land
gave me a life & i've
given it bottle caps. warning:
    choking hazard—mongoose
can't read. immune to snake
venom, susceptible to plastic
bottles. the lake has closed
its eyes—closed its eyes &
swallowed brown water, sprinkled
with plastic bags. warning:
to avoid danger of suffocation,
keep this plastic bag away
from babies & children (& lakes
& oceans & mongooses
& hornbills & turtles &
peacocks & rice fields
& forests & deserts &
& & &)

searching for comfort

suddenly all i can hear   is laughter
needling my ears   & all i feel are
my eyes   fish-bowling / elucidating
becoming   so that they can / anyone
can / tell that my heart   isn't from
here / from the desert   where the dry
feet of humor   spins sand through
air   breathed onto glass / i place
my cracked soles   in a bucket of
water   the same one that my mother
uses / to clear the floor of   earthen
soil that she cradles   in the corner
of her palm   & grows my legs from
on the nights when i cry   on her lap

ode to mehendi

my sister etches a secret into my hand   with the tip
of an arrow   dulled by years of heartache   so it

presses gently to a point   at the furrow of my hand
here   at the corner of my palm anger bows down

to the burning red of mehendi   seeping from her
forehead in the patience   of years   forming

a fox-feather in the web   between my knuckles
she holds my hand close to her face   telling her

heart-child something   that she cannot tell me
i keep my hand pressed against foiled lace   so not

to wrinkle a design   so not to ball up in remission
at my mother's feet with nothing   but a child's

dream in hand   *what if i wasn't an only daughter*
firstborn   *lastborn*   tracing mehendi into

my own hand   late dark nights   over the silent
reading of an english newspaper   now this

curdled buttermilk   leaking through my fingers
grazes my hand so differently   from the cone

in my sister's hand that i wonder   if an arrow
has wicked   & left   my mind

interlude

here lies the girl with fallen knees:
on her collapsed stomach takes
form a butterfly crawling with its
feet on the ground saying
you whose voice
i studied by the warmth of
my mouthpiece you
whom i bore with the heels
of my tired hands
& pressed with my knuckles
washing ashore you
i surrender to the world which
you will learn to take care of
but which may never learn
to take proper care of you

part three: becoming

how to become a beautiful second-language poet

1. try to capture the sun in only one eye / a smile on only one side / tilt my head towards the sky & call me / an artist /

2. say words / are my art while searching / for a paintbrush that is not yet saturated / by dried-up colors & blot / in liquid /

3. take a tablespoon of honey & lemon / mix well at the surface / hold it close to my tonsils, swallow & call it / a goodbye /

4. dissect my heart / at the kitchen table with eyes / of a student / use forceps to squeeze out any remaining honey & find spice-water to use / as a preservative /

5. hold an ant / on the edge of my finger call it a hostage / but let it crawl away onto the neighbor's grass & name it / after my mother /

6. call my mother when / she is working just / to leave a voicemail that says hello / in english but the rest / not in english /

7. write a line in english / because my language is too beautiful for the roughness / of my words / but my lovely english kisses sandpaper with its chapped lips now / smooth /

to milwaukee

thank you
for the lilacs

that you placed
in my hair—

they wilted
last night
by my pillow's
silk.

half-past midnight
& still
there's light

lost mountains
to rivers
i didn't want

i'm afraid
of your claws
that tightly grip

my gentle ears
& refuse
to let go

self-portrait with mother's hands in my heart

some days   i walk down the street
                    imagining my hand holding on to
the hem of your skirt   & hallucinate
your face in a shop window
                    only a mirage   of course
my skin is far too dull   to confuse
                    with the glow of your   ember
your forehead pressed   against
                    mine   my small body curled
against your stomach   i wish
for you to swallow me   the moon in
                    your arms & i in your safekeeping
this   is what i see as i walk towards
                    the end of the world
when we immigrate   this time
together   my heart inside of you
                    your hands   inside of   me

dissimilate

when i mouth   words   to my mother
i half-expect   some   to spill out
of an empty   glass   shattering my throat

with a scarred   tongue   i carve out vowels
and form   shapes   that resemble my
    mother
tongue
        to   replace   missing words that
escape inborn   imprisonment

try not to   *vomit*   she tells me
they will not   *like*   *the scent*
of your   *innards*   *and the taste that*
your language   *leaves*   *on the lingual*
frenulum

in their   *stomach*   it will twist and
turn like a   disease   disowned by
the first-   world   nations

so ensure   *that*   *they will never*
have the   *displeasure*   *of listening*
to a   *language*   *that blatantly*
refuses to   *assimilate*
                              to churn salt
rather than   *milk*

and with that my   mother   remains quiet
and my mother   tongue   laps air

portrait of my tongue as a battleground

it has arrived: in the same fashion as alexander
the great   on horses with swords across rivers
the conqueror the empire   the words that i say
with defeat in my throat are now men falling to
the ground   yearning to be part of the earth

my tongue is an elephant with its trunk in its mouth

i am trying to be gentle to languages that tear
me apart   in two   my hands are my
rivers that he will not cross & to the ignorant
my clasped palms are   where the world
ends

my tongue is a gordian knot   with my fist inside

shopping for a necklace

my mother's hands trace   around my neck
with the cold mouth of an unworn   chain
her hand tightens   & calls upon me
    i want to choose   *carefully*
which necklace   will snake its way around
my hollow neck   & press its head against
my chest   for years to come

the woman at the counter laughs when i say
the necklace   is not light enough
her voice roughened   by all the gold hands
that must have   clasped around her neck
she doesn't know   if i mean to say
it is too heavy   or
it is too dark
but she knows that   i am not from here
her voice reaches   towards my dipping nose
& pinches my lips together   *you're not*
from here   escapes her own lips
in a gold-cut malayalam   i cannot respond
my own lips tightly shut   because only
a necklace can lie   like this   gaping
to be mine   to choke me with the clasp
of my own tongue   because it knows
i remain a stranger

vegetables

the first time my mother sends me   to buy groceries
i come back weeping   *it's just the rain*   i say

but really   it is the vegetables   that i have pared
& eaten with my right hand   the hand that speaks only

malayalam that i cannot translate   these vegetables
i have already named once   cannot rename them

because food is saraswati devi   & i must learn to
buy vegetables   without knowing their english names

that day   my mother feeds me lunch   bitter melon cut
& feathered with spices   snake gourd sliced & curled

at the edges   she places each piece at the center
of my tongue   & readily my mouth curls into a wound

house of spices

in the store   a mother teaches her girl how to live
          she teaches her how   to pick the best okra
by plucking its end   *it looks so much like a lizard*
the girl whispers in her mother tongue   *only*
its tail doesn't fall off   i think to myself & imagine
plucking my tongue out of my mouth   like okra
cut down its center   i fill my own bag with okra
curling outward like a snake's tongue   plucking
the ones my grandmother would   by pressing into
the ripened green   as only her tender hands could
i weigh to the pound with my own hands   *$0.99*
per pound   & add a little spice to round it out
in the corner   the girl drops her okra on the floor
her green tongues weaving together   her mother
screaming   carving a new mouth of tindora
whispering to her daughter   *this is how life tastes*

ode to debate / sometimes, after junior year

when i was younger,
i thought your voice could
cut through my ears.
it made me afraid sometimes,
like the time when
you lifted your eyebrows
at the vulture i brought home.
over time, i learned
to make do:
my fingers rambling &
my voice faltering.
laughter was what
dissolved me—more
            than once—
but it taught me that
voices could sometimes
become their own
vultures.
other times,
you were my only pair
of talons. it was me
grasping tightly, trying not
to fall from the stars
that you let me fashion. no wonder
the seventh point
is so beautifully lopsided.

i take advice from birbal

when asked three questions   i learn
to say the wrong answer   for all three
then   they will praise my wit & forget
that i too   like birbal
am of a different   body

i.   where are you from?
here: although my feet
have never   touched   this
earth   before today
& my hands are too rough
for the land   that sprouts
here

ii.   where are you from, originally?
this city: although it is my mother
& not this city   who carried me
& made me a child   of her tender
arms

iii.   where is your family from?
why must i be made separate
from my family
they live here: with me

orphan tongues

all secrets told,
there is a madness
to the way i speak.

it has been twelve years
since my tongue had melted:
its naivety, cold & fast,

shrunk as it cracked.
my mouth tells no secrets
but my tongue

does without warning.
so it is my ear who
is the mother of my tongue:

she asks for forgiveness
on behalf of her child.
she teaches me how

to apologize,
and most importantly,
how to stop apologizing.

the land

when my mother talks about the place
where she is from she calls it
the *land* in malayalam as though
there is no other land that shadows
her mind there probably isn't
until we reach her land on hot
summer mornings then the *land*
becomes the place where she lost her youth
her innocence her childlike glow & gained
a lifetime of homesickness

ode to temple crowds

in the damp heat of india   my mother wraps the end
of her shawl & tethers it to her waist   she holds

out her finger & says   *here is a lifeline*   as i tongue at
the strand of saffron lodged   between my back teeth

i grab on to her hand   our hands clasping each other
as a prayer unfolds beneath her breath   & she pulls me

through a sea of sweaty bodies that scent   of sacred
incense   set ablaze in the cavity   of my nose

maybe this is where wildfires begin: with bodies stacked
over each other worshipping the divine   but really

each other   wading through monsoon season   only
to be lodged in the mouth of steam   *so this is what*

it means to pray   i say to myself   & glance at my mother
her eyes tightly pressed   & suddenly saffron comes loose

to my father

on sunday,
i picked coconuts
alone for the first time:

i tapped the husk
with my fingers,
curled like yours,

& brushed its hair
like the dolls
i feared.

i shook them vigorously,
the pointed ends,

so you could hear
the rivers
rumbling inside.

as i picked each
coconut, gentle rock,

i remembered
the breakfasts we ate
of coconut shreds.
when i was young,

& when i turned old,
i placed the shreds aside
for you to pick.

you opened your palms,
fronds of

a coconut tree,

& revealed the husk
of a ripened seed.

each coconut
split open,
each river set free,
you became
a mountain

to father
an ocean.

part four: rebellion

brewing

in rebellion i first call myself human
& wait for them to correct me
slick back my tongue with steel wool
fall roughly & scrape my teeth so that
they become blue as the night sky
where i harpoon for stars
in rebellion i last call myself immortal
& wait for them to line their mouths
with white silk caught on my nails
& make no response in fear
bare my knuckles in the earth only
to tarnish beauty to discover what
really is mine

ghazal for all the world

what will become of a burning world
when ice melts her feet on this burning world?

the mountains smile in delightless pain:
they know the taste of a churning world.

a breeze morphs, whisks away his son,
before he jolts on this turning world.

an apple that rolls at the base of a tree
is tossed far beyond this learning world.

here, a parade to honor a shining girl,
there, a star and a yearning world.

a galaxy dissolves its own withering face:
no longer with bliss of a returning world.

laxmi plaza

indian grocery store featuring
a selection of produce,
frozen food, dry goods, sweets
& seasonings.
// orlando, florida

back then, laxmi
was still a young girl,
only school age,
with her hair plaited
in two slanted braids
& her eyes circled
in charcoal-black.
her classmates fussed
over the spelling
of her name:
they called it
fresh, new age,
modern even,

like the imported
white chocolate
at the city bazaar.
in the afternoons,
she ate two samosas (३०₹)
at the bakery, almost
fresh,
& practiced the english
she learned
at her modern school.
on sundays,
she listened to stories

that her uncle brought,
from venice,
from london,
from west
of the berlin wall.
she dreamt
even further,
halfway across
the world.
at twenty, laxmi
packed her bags,

off to a foreign land.
she carried incense,
samosas, frozen
shrikhand, &
henna from
her mother's drawer.
once a week,
she called home ($1.50)

to talk of school
& her new business:
okra ($2/lb) &
incense ($2) &
freezer-grade pedas ($5.99).
a few years after,
she imported
mangoes ($6.99/box) from
the other hemisphere:
same story,
different taste.
to her children,
she told a story

of a world—
a sharp right
off of the orange
blossom trail,
where girls
wrapped in saris
came to laugh &
thread their
eyebrows &
munch
on samosas ($1.50).

revolution in my mind

on summer nights   heat turns
my feet to wax & i make
promises that i cannot keep

i tell myself that i will come back
to this moment & this place
that has turned its aged face away

this moment is shrouded in someone
else's memories of my own
foremothers & memory has swallowed me

i am becoming the food my mother
made me: my skin
boils away as grains of rice

i begin   to make something out
of a banishment at birth
with hands all made out of henna

birds of a country

& though i am now fifteen
          i imagine myself   drawing breaths
in a country   that still calls me child
that still bundles my goddess-name
          in its labored arms
& sends me a black eagle   wishing me luck
in the country   where i was born
          where my name means nothing   more
than three letters   than an actress i've never been
          where only bald eagles fly
& are loved   they never migrate this far
& wreak havoc
          they only teethe on my finger   like a child
          they only tear apart my heart   like a man
in haste   i search for the perfect name
     but it never responds

border violence

this is where i draw a line
i say to the words
that tear me apart in two

& now i will tell you there
are words in my fists—
carefully hand-picked

correctly spelled because these
are not true mistakes
just fables of mankind

it is not the words it is
the people who laugh
at splitting bodies from afar

those are the people it is them
whom i ask who *are* you
from where have you built

your arrogance is it fenced
is it concrete does it split me
vertically or horizontally

hand in mouth

at the top
of the food chain,
there are men

who do not eat,
but devour,
the earth.

they bare their
chiseled teeth, in all
its bleached appeal,
at the sun, the moon &

the soil in their hands.
often, they say
that mouths are empty—
with their own mouths bursting

at the corners
as their mothers
try to escape.

their hands
are mouths, gasping
for air. when pried open,
they are empty &

they give nothing
to the hand
that is raised.
only mountains

may close their

wailing jaws,
the peak lodged

between a tooth &
a tongue.

how they say

my mother turns up the volume   of a video
that loops   & loops   until
it is never over   the rhythm of words
hypnotizes us   so that i cannot distinguish
        whether my tongue has caved   or
my words have caved   how they say it
matters even more   than how i spell it
i am careful to say it   where the sun sets

independence

my grandmother tells me a story   in which
she is only seven   a time when she
walked miles to school barefoot   visiting
a temple on the way each day   she
tells me of early morning baths   in cold
water-wells   diving feet-first   she says
these   *were my happiest days*
it is 1947   & my grandmother bathes
in the glory   of her country's independence
she tells of a day   in the heat of august
when she walked through the streets
waving a flag   clutched in her small hands
& ran home   her feet filling cracks in the
stone   she says   *these were the days*
i felt pride   & sinks back into her breath

friday night (ii)

slowly   i'm growing too old
    to be housed in my own body
my smooth legs are too long for
the couch   & the television presses
    my knees to my chest
my right eye is filled with
excuses   & my eyebrow is growing
    longer each day
my mother asks me to buy
a coconut from the store
i douse it in water & trace
its orbits
    this is where i am, this
    is where i should be
my father calls on me to visit
the neighbor—an empty lake
with a gaping mouth
        & i nod—
tomorrow
even the man on the phone asks
whether i've grown into my voice
or if it has grown on to me
i say that i've only begun to knit
myself & put down the phone
    before he's done
on friday nights   sleeping makes me
homesick   & my mother's arms
are my only home
their only home is missing from
    my dreams

tillana

a woman on the street tells me
that i have the body of a dancer

my mouth leaps
                    into rhythms

          maybe the posture

is a little bent

[mispronunciations]

i try to pull out a chameleon's
tongue from inside my throat,
change the color, change it all
before another
          [mispronunciation]
leaves my colorless mouth

instead i find my mother tongue
stuck inside my throat, a lump
forgotten only by me
& i find a desire, tucked away,
to strangle her and choke myself
before another
          [mispronunciation]
escapes without explanation

i am afraid that i have stained
the english that i speak
that it yearns to be bleached
in cold sand

i watch my mother chug down
womanhood,
let it slide through the grip of her
mother tongue,
into the stomach of america
          [& her mispronunciations]

how to avoid falling in love with my own writing

it's simple: my words are not
my words   my words
were carved   by some man
biting a smile between   his
teeth   ripping apart   scathing
a sword   from under his
tongue   dripping   with
blood of my people   martyrs
to broken words   & no
questions   just quests why
would i love this writing   if it
cost me   my people   my
blood my songs   my memories
my words   in another language

a lesson on colonization & genocide

there is a misconception   that blood
does not leak   through these surfaces

that these colors absorb   the burning
red of blood   & leave you   a river

of obedience   this   is not a science
science says   that blood leaks

through   brown   cloth the same way
that blood leaks   through white cloth

& still this   is not   a geography
this   is a recipe for alienation   that

does not even require a second planet
instead you make aliens out of people

in your own world   but   you cannot
change the viscosity of blood   you

can only make us bleed   you cannot
make our blood   this   is an identity

what if i realized that my blood tastes
the same as your blood   & what if

i made   my own recipe   from this
would you hide   your leaking blood

like you made us do

akbar & birbal eat together

they say   that king akbar once begged
for food & still   he saved some for birbal
a king never trusted a man so well   as akbar
did birbal   they ate together   laughed together
men of two different robes   & men
of two different prayers

they say that birbal died in a military ambush
men rebelled against akbar   & birbal
rebelled against men
his body   was not found   it was just one
among thousands   of wingless crows
akbar did not eat for two days   maybe
he stared up at the sky   or
maybe he was saving it all
for birbal

postlude

legend has it that the end of the world   shall arrive
on a white horse   as every good war hero
the end of the world shall arrive   just moments
before evil has won   to save us from ourselves
by simply destroying us   & the best part
is that humankind will never win   whether or not
the end comes   so why do we resist change
harbor fear
& whittle smoke
if it is we   who mothered rebellion
against the inevitable

Acknowledgments

To my family—Amma, Achan, Ammamma, as well as my cousins and extended family, who have taught me what family means.

To all those who have shared their wisdom with me—educators, mentors, and my high school debate coach.

And to the South Asian Diaspora, for which I have written this collection.

Some of these poems have appeared previously in the following publications:

Euphony Journal: "the creation of a language"

Mikrokosmos Journal: "coming home"

Glass: A Journal of Poetry: "out"

SAND Journal Berlin: "spoken language"

The Cincinnati Review miCRo: "trusting the birds"

Jaggery Lit: "ode to mehendi"

Ruminate Magazine: "ode to temple crowds"

National Poetry Quarterly: "independence"

The Rumpus: "my grandmother's jewelry," "vegetables," "a lesson on colonization & genocide"

Brain Mill Press Voices: "shopping for a necklace," "[mispronunciations]"

Ms. Magazine: "the universe, a woman"

Iris Magazine: "the universe, a woman"

Peach Magazine: "girl growing up in the south enters the midwest," "ode to debate/sometimes, after junior year" (as "sometimes, after junior year"), "leaving milwaukee"

Skipping Stones Magazine: "giving a mongoose a plastic bottle," "orphan tongues," "border violence"

About the Author

Uma Menon is a sixteen-year-old high school student and author from Winter Park, Florida.

Her acclaimed writing has been nominated twice for the Pushcart Prize and appeared in over three dozen different publications, including *The Huffington Post*, *The Progressive*, *The Rumpus*, and *Orlando Sentinel*. She has also received the 2019 Lee Bennett Hopkins Award from the Florida State Poets Association and won the National High School Poetry Contest. Uma was named a 2019 National Poetry Month Editor's Pick Poet by Brain Mill Press and a 2020 National YoungArts Winner in Writing. Her first chapbook was published by Zoetic Press. *Hands for Language* is her debut book and was shortlisted by the 2019 International Erbacce-Prize.

As a social justice advocate, Uma is engaged in issues such as educational accessibility, gun control, net neutrality, and representation of marginalized communities. She is a student leader for College Board's Access to Education Council and an Action Fellow for the Alliance for Climate Education. In high school, she was also the captain of her school's debate team and a nationally-ranked debater. Uma is the first Youth Fellow for the International Human Rights Art Festival (IHRAF), through which position she works to amplify youth voices in social justice discourse.

Uma was invited to the 2019 State of the Union by US Congresswoman Stephanie Murphy in recognition of her writing on youth activism, making her one of the youngest guests in the event's history. She was also selected to the 2020 US Senate Youth Program, where she will serve as one of two Youth Senators from each state. Uma was named by Kudumbam Magazine as one of the 100 Most Influential Women of Malayali Origin in 2018.

Uma graduated from Winter Park High School's International Baccalaureate Program in 2020 and will attend Princeton University in the fall.